MW01106428

FORESTS

TREES & WOOD

Dave,
You are a great teacher and helped me get off to a good start on my career in forestry. We hope you enjoy this book and someday get to read it to your grandchildren.

Thank you

Jim Livingston

Mary Livingston

 Red Tail Publishing, P.O. Box 151, Palo Cedro, CA 96073.

ISBN 0-9635757-0-8 • Printed in U.S.A. • First Printing 1993

FORESTS
TREES & WOOD
Where Wood Comes From

By Tim and Mary Livingston
Illustrations by Tim Livingston

RED TAIL PUBLISHING, PALO CEDRO, CALIFORNIA

This book is dedicated to
Christopher and Stephen.

Photo by Mary Livingston

Many forestry professionals choose their careers so they can positively influence the ways we participate with nature.

It is for our children that this example of good stewardship must be set, for they are the forestry professionals of tomorrow.

Our forests give us many things.

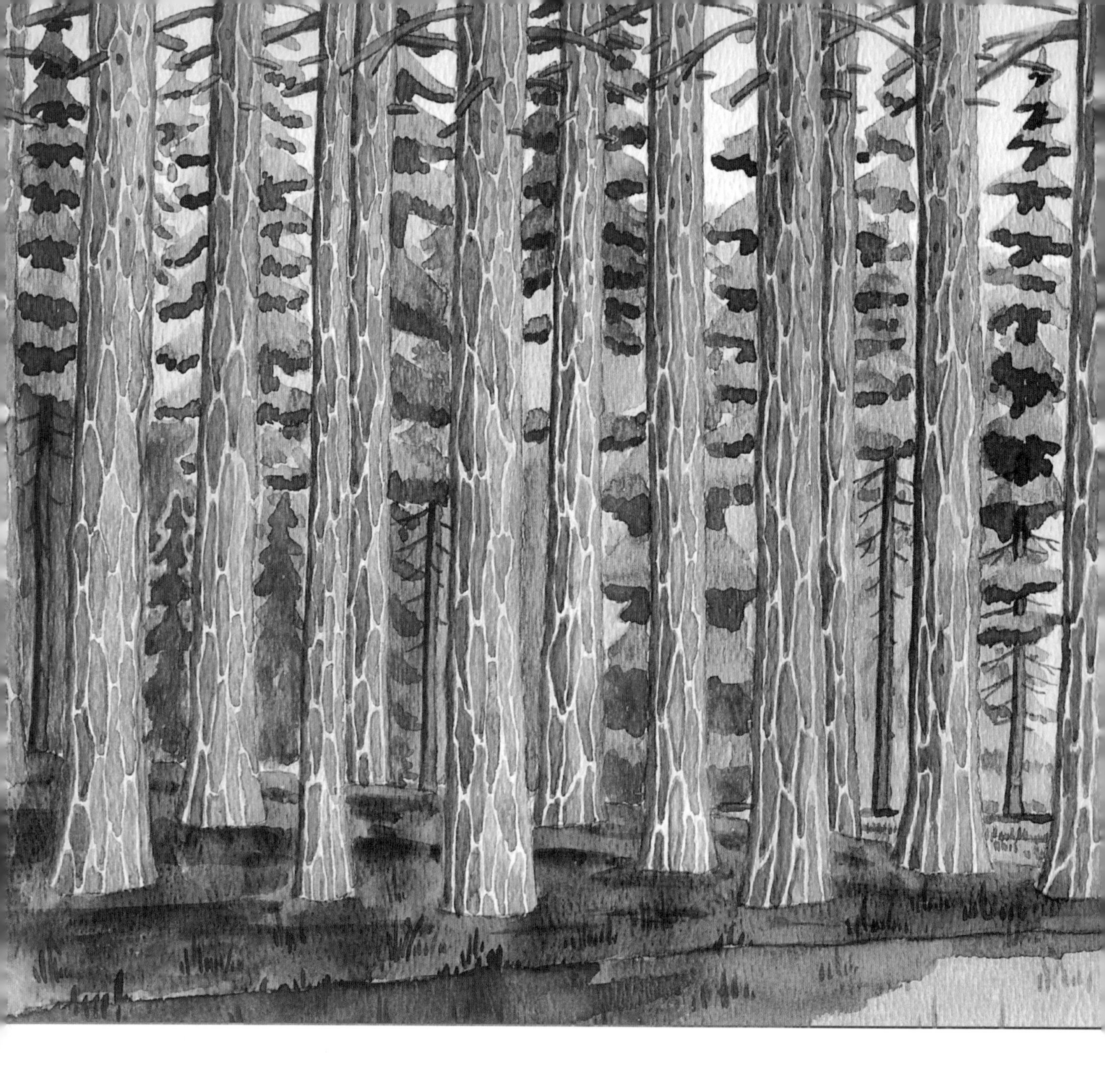

They have beauty, wild animals, water and trees.

Trees in the forest give us wood.

Foresters make a plan to care for the forest and its creatures before using any trees for wood. By knowing about the animals that live in the forest people can even improve wildlife habitat.

Other important things in the forest that are protected under this plan are soil, water, and archeological sites. Past and future land uses are also considered.

The forest plan is followed when marking trees for wood.

Sometimes trees are removed because they are sick or dying, crooked or broken, or just because they need more room to grow. These foresters are marking the trees that are too crowded.

All forest workers follow the forest plan while harvesting wood. These timber fallers use special tools and safety equipment to manufacture logs.

Loggers use special tractors called skidders to take the logs to a landing.

At the landing log loaders load the logs onto trucks.

Logging trucks take the logs to the sawmill.

At the sawmill loaders unload the logs. A person called a scaler measures them.

A crane stores some of the logs in decks.

In the mill logs are sawn into lumber.

People stack the lumber in units.

Fork lifts load the lumber onto trucks

and trains to be hauled to factories and stores.

People use wood to make homes, tables, chairs,

books, toys and many other things we use everyday.

Cogeneration plants make electricity from wood scraps, chips and sawdust.

Chipped wood is also made into pulp for paper. People try to use all parts of a log.

Back in the forest people carefully use fire, one of nature's tools, to clean up slash and debris. This helps prevent forest fires and adds nutrients to the soil.

Foresters spread straw and plant grass to keep soil from washing away.

They plant new trees so we will always have trees.

These are some of the ways to take care of our forests.

A healthy forest gives us beauty, wild animals, water and trees.

By taking care of our forests they will continue to grow and give us many things.